KT-382-588

First published in Great Britain in 2002 by Bloomsbury Publishing Plc
38 Soho Square, London, W1D 3HB
This paperback edition first published in 2003

A CIP catalogue record of this book is available from the British Library

ISBN 0 7475 6117 6

Printed in Hong Kong by C&C Offset

3 5 7 9 10 8 6 4 2

THIS BLOOMSBURY BOOK

BELONGS TO

Busy Night

Ross Collins

BLOOMSBURY
CHILDREN'S
BOOKS

"Just five more minutes," yawned Ben.
"Pleeaase, Mum..."

"Look at you." said Ben's mum.
"Barely enough energy to play with that
loose tooth of yours.
Get off to bed - pronto."

Ben reluctantly crawled upstairs to bed.

Ben washed his face,

gingerly brushed his teeth,

put on the bunny pyjamas
which nobody knew about,
and got under the covers.

CLICK! Out went the light, and so did Ben.
The clock in the hall struck the hour
and all was quiet.

Except,

CRREEAAAK, the window was opening...

A strange little figure hauled his huge pockets into Ben's room.
He poked Ben's nose and seemingly satisfied, began to softly sing.

"The Sandman's here, the Sandman's here,
Boys and girls have nothing to fear.
With a sprinkling of sand around your bed,
Lovely dreams will be popping right into your head.
Of peaches and cream and liquorice shoes,
Of lemonade navels and ... "

"**O I !**" interrupted a disgruntled voice.

"GET A MOVE ON, SANDY PANTS!"

It was the tooth Fairy.
And she was late.
"SOME OF US HAVE
TEETH TO COLLECT."

The Sandman
stopped sprinkling his sand.

"Quiet you," he whispered,
"the Creature is only dozing
and I haven't finished my song yet."

"LOOK, SANDWICH," said the fairy,
"I'VE GOT A WHOLE GOBFUL OF MOLARS TO
GRAB BY MIDNIGHT AND YOU'RE HOLDING UP
THE SCHEDULE."

"Shhhhh!" said the Sandman,
"We mustn't wake the ..."

"WOOOOOOOOOOO!"
interrupted a new voice.

It was the Ghosts.

WOOOO RATTLE RATTLE!

There was a pause, then they said it again.
"WOOOO. RATTLE RATTLE."
"IT'S A-HAUNTIN' TIME." they wailed,
"RUN IN TERROR!"

"BOG OFF!" said the Tooth Fairy.

"Pipe down, chaps," said the Sandman.

"Perhaps if we formed a queue ... "

"I've not even seen an incisor yet," said the Tooth Fairy.

"WOOOO ... " started the Ghosts, but they were interrupted

by a loud raspberry. "THBBTHBPTHH!"

"WHAAT WAAS THAAATT?"
whispered the ghosts.
"It came from under the bed,"
gulped the Sandman.
"THBBTHBP! SLAP!
GURGLE! BLABTHH!"
went a gurgly voice.

"I AM THE THING-UNDER-THE-BED AND I COME
OUT ... JUST ABOUT NOW! BFHT!" gargled the voice.
"What do you look like?" asked the Tooth Fairy.
"WHATEVER GIVES YOU THE WILLIES," came the voice.
"TONIGHT I WILL BE GREENY PURPLE.
NOW GO AWAY!"

Everybody was a bit scared
by the Thing-Under-the-Bed,
especially the Ghosts.
"NOOBODY TOLD US ABOUT
HIIMMMMMM," they said.
"Look, maybe we should
draw straws," suggested the Sandman.
"Just one wisdom tooth
and I'm off," said the Tooth Fairy.
"THBTHPBT! RASP!"
said the Thing-Under-the-Bed.
"I'VE GOT TENTACLES! AND BIG..."
CRUUMMPF!
He was interrupted by a noise in the fireplace.

"HO! HO! HO!" came a booming voice.
It was Santa Claus.

Everybody looked at him, then at each other, then back at Santa.
"IT'S NOT EVEN CHRISTMAS!!" they all yelled together.
"ISN'T IT?" asked Santa.
"NOOO!!"
"Blast those elves!" said Santa. "Second time I've fallen for that this year."
Even the Thing-Under-the-Bed came out for a peek.
"LOOK, EVERYONE!" shouted the Tooth Fairy.
"HE'S SOFT! GET HIM!"

Everybody jumped on the Thing-Out-from-Under-the-Bed and started arguing.

WHO WANTS A TOOTH LOOSENED?

WOOOOO!

MUNCH!

OH DEAR!

BFFTHT!

KEEP THE NOISE DOWN CHAPS!

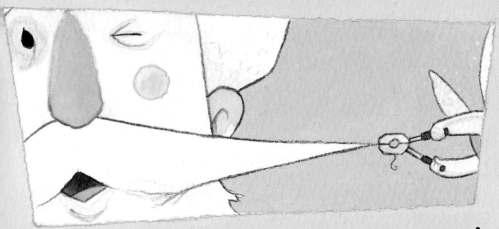

THIS ISN'T AT ALL CHRISTMASSY!

BLECH!

JUST ONE MOLAR!

WOOOMF!

I WAS HERE FIRST!

But then they were all interrupted. "AH-HEM!"

SOME OF US ARE TRYING TO GET SOME SLEEP ROUND HERE!

So they did.

"So what are we going to do now?"
"I hear Mary Cuthbertson across the street has a
loose milk tooth."
"Does she like tentacles?"
"**RATTLE.**"

"Is it Christmas yet?"